Santa's
Kiwi Holiday

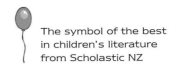

The symbol of the best
in children's literature
from Scholastic NZ

Published in 2005 by Scholastic New Zealand Limited
Private Bag 94407, Greenmount, Auckland 1730, New Zealand

Scholastic Australia Pty Limited
PO Box 579, Gosford, NSW 2250, Australia

ISBN 1-86943-706-3

National Library of New Zealand Cataloguing-in-Publication Data

Farrer, Maria, 1962-
Santa's Kiwi holiday / by Maria Farrer ; illustrated by Deborah Hinde.
ISBN 1-86943-706-3
[1. Santa Claus—Fiction. 2. Christmas—Fiction. 3. Holidays—
Fiction. 4. New Zealand—Fiction.] I. Hinde, Deborah, 1957-
II. Title.
NZ823.3—dc 22

9 8 7 6 5 4 3 2 1   5 6 7 8 9 / 0

Illustrations completed using acrylic paints

Publishing team: Christine Dale, Penny Scown and Annette Bisman
Layout by Book Design Limited, Christchurch, New Zealand
Typeset in Utopia 20/30pt

Santa's Kiwi Holiday

WRITTEN BY
Maria Farrer

ILLUSTRATED BY
Deborah Hinde

SCHOLASTIC
AUCKLAND SYDNEY NEW YORK LONDON TORONTO
MEXICO CITY NEW DELHI HONG KONG

The Arctic's cold in mid December.
It's where poor Santa lives, remember?
He's always busy – never slacks –
it's hard work filling Christmas sacks.

He works all day and half the night
to get our toys and gifts just right.
And as each Christmas comes a-knocking,
he's ready with our Christmas stocking.

NORTH POLE

But Santa's feeling not his best.
"I'm tired," he says, "I need a rest.
It's time I had a break away.
I think I'll go on holiday!"

He scans the globe for where to go.
Sea and sun, not ice and snow.
Mountains, rivers, native bush …
he gives the globe another push.

And then his heart begins to race!
New Zealand looks the perfect place.
He packs his bag without delay,
and soon is ready on his sleigh.

Up and up! To trade winds high.
Reindeer pounding cloudless sky,
across the earth and oceans proud,
down to 'the land of the long white cloud'.

Santa arrives at break of day.
The beauty takes his breath away!
Crystal seas and forests green;
the best that he has ever seen.

The reindeer, they need food and sleep.
He leaves them grazing with some sheep.
Ready now, to have some fun!
He strips his coat off in the sun.

No belt to hold his ample belly,
it wobbles round just like a jelly.
"Goodness gracious, what a state!
I'd better lose some of this weight."

It isn't really that surprising –
Santa's not known for exercising.
He knows he should get fit and strong,
for Christmas Eve is hard and long.

BEACH ACCESS

So down the beach dear Santa jogs,
dressed only in his swimming togs.
He feels alive, and young and free –
the way you do beside the sea.

He doesn't swim for very long,
to do too much would be quite wrong,
and with ideas of getting tanned,
he lays himself upon the sand.

His pure white skin, so bright and dazzling,
is not prepared for such a frazzling.
Before too long he feels the burn;
the sun – it gives him quite a turn.

The kids, they ask him,
"Where's your cap?
When on the beach it's
slip, slop, slap."

So Santa buys some
good sunscreen,
a shirt and hat of holly green.

He has a shower, and once he's dried,
he goes and buys a tourist guide.
There is so much to see and do,
he makes a plan of what to view.

Te Papa, the Treaty of Waitangi,
a Maori marae, a tasty hangi;
caves with glow-worms shining bright,
each a twinkling fairy light.

This bubbling, sulphur wonderland
he finds quite hard to understand.
So different from his land of ice –
he's sure it doesn't smell
so nice.

He buys himself a history book,
to read the tales of Captain Cook.

He scallops in the scallop grounds,

and fishes for snapper in the Sounds.

Then Santa thinks he'll try some tramping,
and do a bit of Kiwi camping.
He buys a tent and huge backpack,
and sets off down the Heaphy Track.

Heaphy Track

BrownsHut   5mins

He swims with dolphins,

watches whales,

tries some mountain-biking trails,

He flies his sleigh around Mount Cook,

HIGH PEAK

and finds the glaciers
worth a look.

He covers every inch of ground;
takes a boat on Milford Sound,

speeds in jetboats close to rocks ...

and swings across a flying fox.

His holiday is nearly through
but there's still so much to see and do.
"I will be very sad to go …
New Zealand is such fun, you know."

But one last thing, one final treat …
they tie the cord around his feet …
the biggest drop he's ever seen …
he jumps into the deep ravine!

The reindeer hide their big brown eyes,
"What will we do if Santa dies?"
They fear that he might hit his head.
Poor Rudolf's nose goes brighter red!

Upside-down, to sounds of cheers,
he chuckles as he reappears,
"Chimneys won't be such a bump
now I've learned to bungy jump!"

And on that cheery, happy note,
Santa fastens belt and coat.
He leaps upon his trusty sleigh,
for now he must be on his way.

He raises his hand to wave goodbye
and heads back to the northern sky.
He does not really want to leave,
But he'll be back …

on Christmas Eve.